W9-BLJ-767

The Boxcar Children Mysteries

THE BOXCAR CHILDREN
SURPRISE ISLAND
THE YELLOW HOUSE
  MYSTERY
MYSTERY RANCH
MIKE'S MYSTERY
BLUE BAY MYSTERY
THE WOODSHED MYSTERY
THE LIGHTHOUSE MYSTERY
MOUNTAIN TOP MYSTERY
SCHOOLHOUSE MYSTERY
CABOOSE MYSTERY
HOUSEBOAT MYSTERY
SNOWBOUND MYSTERY
TREE HOUSE MYSTERY
BICYCLE MYSTERY
MYSTERY IN THE SAND
MYSTERY BEHIND THE WALL
BUS STATION MYSTERY
BENNY UNCOVERS A MYSTERY
THE HAUNTED CABIN
  MYSTERY
THE DESERTED LIBRARY
  MYSTERY
THE ANIMAL SHELTER
  MYSTERY
THE OLD MOTEL MYSTERY
THE MYSTERY OF THE HIDDEN
  PAINTING
THE AMUSEMENT PARK
  MYSTERY
THE MYSTERY OF THE
  MIXED-UP ZOO
THE CAMP-OUT MYSTERY
THE MYSTERY GIRL
THE MYSTERY CRUISE
THE DISAPPEARING FRIEND
  MYSTERY
THE MYSTERY OF THE SINGING
  GHOST
MYSTERY IN THE SNOW
THE PIZZA MYSTERY
THE MYSTERY HORSE

THE MYSTERY AT THE DOG
  SHOW
THE CASTLE MYSTERY
THE MYSTERY OF THE LOST
  VILLAGE
THE MYSTERY ON THE ICE
THE MYSTERY OF THE
  PURPLE POOL
THE GHOST SHIP MYSTERY
THE MYSTERY IN
  WASHINGTON, DC
THE CANOE TRIP MYSTERY
THE MYSTERY OF THE HIDDEN
  BEACH
THE MYSTERY OF THE MISSING
  CAT
THE MYSTERY AT SNOWFLAKE
  INN
THE MYSTERY ON STAGE
THE DINOSAUR MYSTERY
THE MYSTERY OF THE STOLEN
  MUSIC
THE MYSTERY AT THE BALL
  PARK
THE CHOCOLATE SUNDAE
  MYSTERY
THE MYSTERY OF THE HOT
  AIR BALLOON
THE MYSTERY BOOKSTORE
THE PILGRIM VILLAGE
  MYSTERY
THE MYSTERY OF THE STOLEN
  BOXCAR
THE MYSTERY IN THE CAVE
THE MYSTERY ON THE TRAIN
THE MYSTERY AT THE FAIR
THE MYSTERY OF THE LOST
  MINE
THE GUIDE DOG MYSTERY
THE HURRICANE MYSTERY
THE PET SHOP MYSTERY
THE MYSTERY OF THE
  SECRET MESSAGE

THE GHOST OF THE CHATTERING BONES

created by
GERTRUDE CHANDLER WARNER

Illustrated by Robert Papp

ALBERT WHITMAN & Company
Morton Grove, IL

The Ghost of the Chattering Bones
created by Gertrude Chandler Warner;
illustrated by Robert Papp.

ISBN 0-8075-0875-6 (hardcover)
ISBN 0-8075-0874-8 (paperback)

Cover art by Robert Papp.

For more information about Albert Whitman & Company,
visit our web site at www.albertwhitman.com.

Contents

THE GHOST OF THE CHATTERING BONES

CHAPTER 1

The Haunted Bridge

"What kind of mystery is it, Mrs. McGregor?" asked six-year-old Benny. The youngest Alden couldn't keep still. He was bouncing up and down with excitement in the backseat of the family van.

Mrs. McGregor, who was sitting up front beside Grandfather Alden, looked over her shoulder and smiled. "It's Norah's story to tell, Benny," she said. "Not mine."

Henry gave his little brother a playful nudge. "Hold your horses, Benny," he said.

"It won't be long before we're at Eton Place." At fourteen, Henry was the oldest of the Aldens.

"I guess I can hold my horses a little bit longer," said Benny. He didn't like to wait.

Norah Eton, a good friend of the Aldens' housekeeper, had invited Mrs. McGregor and the four Alden children to come for a visit in the country. There was an old mystery that needed solving, and Henry, Jessie, Violet, and Benny were eager to hear all about it. There was nothing the Aldens liked better than a mystery. And together they'd managed to solve quite a few.

Twelve-year-old Jessie looked up from the map she was studying. "We make a left at the next road, Grandfather," she told him. Jessie was the best map reader in the family. She always knew how to get where they were going.

"Oh, now I remember!" Mrs. McGregor nodded. "It's been so long since I've been out this way, my memory's a bit foggy."

"How long has it been, Mrs. McGregor?" Grandfather Alden asked, as they turned off the highway onto a gravel road full of twists and turns.

"Let me see, now . . . Norah's great-niece, Pam, was just a toddler the last time I saw her," said Mrs. McGregor. She thought for a moment "Now she would be about Violet's age."

At the mention of her name, ten-year-old Violet turned away from the window. "Will Pam be staying with her great-aunt Norah all summer?" she wanted to know.

"Oh, I imagine so," Mrs. McGregor answered. "She usually does. You see, her parents own an antique store in the city. They spend their summers traveling all over the country hunting for treasures."

Benny's eyebrows shot up. "Treasures?"

"Interesting old things to sell in their store," explained Mrs. McGregor. "They stop at every flea market and swap meet they can find."

That sounded like fun to Benny. "Why doesn't Pam go along?"

"Travel can be tiring," put in Grandfather, who often went away on business.

"Yes, indeed," agreed Mrs. McGregor.

"I imagine Pam would much rather spend her summers with her great-aunt Norah."

"That makes sense," said Henry.

Mrs. McGregor went on, "When Norah and I were young, we loved exploring Eton Place—all the fields and the streams and the woods. The property's been in the Eton family for a long time. As a matter of fact," she added, "Norah's putting together a history of the Eton family. She even hired a college student to help with the research."

"That must be interesting," said Jessie. "I'd like to put together a history of the Alden family sometime."

Benny tapped on his sister's shoulder to get her attention. "Don't forget to mention Watch, Jessie," he reminded her. Watch was the family dog.

"Oh, Benny!" Jessie laughed. "I'd never forget Watch."

"How about our boxcar?" asked Benny.

"I'd never forget our boxcar, either," Jessie told her little brother. "Our old home is an important part of our family history."

After their parents died, Jessie, Henry,

Benny, and Violet had run away. They found an old boxcar in the woods and stayed there for a while. Then James Alden found his grandchildren and brought them to live with him in his big white house in Greenfield. He even gave the boxcar a special place in the backyard. The children often used their former home as a clubhouse.

"I'm glad I brought my camera along," said Violet. "We can take pictures of our trip to go in our family history."

James Alden smiled into the rear view mirror. "Photos are a great way to keep a record of the times."

"I wonder what they did in the olden days," Jessie said thoughtfully, "before cameras were invented."

"They didn't have cameras back then?" Benny sounded surprised.

Violet shook her head. "Not until the 1820s." Violet knew a lot about photography. It was one of her hobbies.

"You're becoming a real expert, Violet," said Henry.

"Thanks, Henry." Violet beamed. "But

I still have a lot to learn."

Grandfather spotted a small gas station. He pulled up close to the gas pumps. A woman with gray streaks in her dark hair came over to the car.

"Fill 'er up?" the woman asked with a friendly smile. She was wearing blue overalls with the name DARLENE embroidered across the front.

Grandfather nodded. "You read my mind."

While Darlene filled the tank, the children hopped out of the car. They set to work washing the windows and the headlights.

"You folks on vacation?" Darlene asked them.

Jessie nodded. "We're spending a week in the country."

"Oh?"

"At Eton Place," Benny added.

As Darlene replaced the cap on the gas tank, she lowered her voice. "A word of advice," she said. "Don't go fishing from the old stone bridge. Some say it's haunted." Her eyes twinkled but her voice was serious.

The children were so surprised by Darlene's word that they were speechless. Before they had a chance to ask any questions, Grandfather had paid the bill and they were on their way again.

"Eton Place sounds a little . . . spooky," Benny said as they drove along.

"You don't believe there's really a ghost, do you?" Henry asked in his sensible way.

"Um, no," Benny said. But he didn't sound too sure.

Violet added, "Darlene was just teasing."

"I imagine she was talking about the ghost of the Chattering Bones," put in Mrs. McGregor.

The children all looked at their housekeeper in surprise. "The ghost of the what?" said Benny, his eyes round. "Did you say—"

"Oh, look!" Mrs. McGregor broke in, as the car rounded a curve. "There's the mailbox!"

Benny craned his neck. "Where?" he asked. He had been thinking about chattering bones. They were a scary thought.

Mrs. McGregor pointed to the side of the road. Sure enough, up ahead was a mailbox set atop a post. The shiny gold lettering on the side of the mailbox read: ETON PLACE.

Grandfather turned the station wagon into a long driveway that wound through the trees. They slowed to a stop when they came to a big plum-colored house with a large porch. On one side was an orchard. On the other, a flower garden.

"Oh, a purple house!" Violet cried with delight as she scooted sideways out of the wide backseat. Purple was Violet's favorite color. She almost always wore something purple or violet.

"Yes, the house has always been plum-colored," said Mrs. McGregor as Henry opened the car door for her. "Thanks to Meg Plum."

As Grandfather lifted the suitcases out of the car, Jessie noticed a tall, silver-haired woman in a flowery-blue sundress standing near the orchard. She was talking to a man in a business suit. As if feeling Jessie's eyes on her, the woman suddenly looked over.

"Margaret!" The tall woman rushed towards Mrs. McGregor. "How wonderful to see you!"

"It's been too long," said Mrs. McGregor, returning her friend's warm hug.

"And this fine-looking group must be the Alden family!" Norah Eton said.

Mrs. McGregor proudly introduced everyone. "Welcome to Eton Place!" Norah said, a smile spreading across her face. "I can't wait for you to meet my niece. I know she'll enjoy your company."

"We're looking forward to meeting Pam," said Jessie, speaking for them all.

"Guess what, Mrs. Eton?" Benny put in. He was still thinking about the mystery.

"What, Benny?"

"We're pretty good at tracking down clues," he told her proudly.

"So I've heard," said Norah. "I'll tell you all about the old mystery after dinner, Benny. But you have to promise me one thing."

"All right," said Benny. "What is it?"

"You must call me Norah."

"Okay, Norah," agreed Benny. "It's a deal!"

Just then, a voice boomed out. "I'm Spence Morton." The man in the business suit walked toward the group and put out his hand for Grandfather to shake. "I hope you're not here about the bridge, too," he said. "I made a fair offer, but I'll go higher if necessary."

Henry, Jessie, Violet, and Benny looked at each other in bewilderment. Was this the same bridge Darlene had mentioned?

Spence Morton went on, "I was passing through town and happened to pick up a local paper." He pulled a newspaper out from under his arm and thumped a finger under a picture of an old stone bridge. "This is exactly what I've been looking for!" he told them, his eyes glittering behind gold-rimmed glasses. "My wife takes great pride in her English garden," he added, "and this charming bridge will be perfect for the stream that runs through it."

"That bridge is not for sale," Norah stated icily. "As I said before, you're wasting your time."

The man did not look pleased to hear this. "Everything has a price tag," he insisted.

"We'll see about that." Norah's mouth was set in a thin, hard line.

"Mark my words," said Spence Morton, "I'll do whatever it takes to get what I want." With that, he turned and walked away.

Norah sighed. "Every time I turn around lately, there's Spence Morton. Yesterday I found him measuring my bridge! Can you believe it?"

Mrs. McGregor shook her head. "The nerve!"

"He isn't a bad person, but . . . " Norah stopped and let out a long sigh.

"But," finished Grandfather, "he just won't take no for an answer."

Norah nodded slowly. "I wish now I'd never let the newspaper do that write-up on my bridge." Then, changing the subject, she added, "Will you join us for a late dinner, James? There's plenty to go around."

"Thanks, Norah," he said, "but the sun's already going down, and I still have some business to take care of."

Grandfather gave a cheery honk as he drove away. Everyone waved, then headed toward the plum-colored house.

Mrs. McGregor looked around as they stepped inside. She smiled at Norah. "I see you've made some changes," she said.

"Yes, I finally got around to fixing the house up a bit," said Norah. As she led the way to the stairs, she shook her head. "But what a mess! Walls torn down…floorboards pulled up. This place was a real disaster area for a while."

Upstairs, a room with plum-patterned wallpaper was waiting for Mrs. McGregor, another with fan-shaped windows for Violet and Jessie. A third bedroom with twin beds and fringed blue bedspreads was just right for Henry and Benny.

"We've been keeping dinner warm for you," Norah told them. "Anybody hungry?"

Benny waved his hand in the air. "I am!

I am!" he cried, to no one's surprise. The youngest Alden was always hungry.

Norah laughed. "Well, come on down as soon as you've settled in."

It didn't take the Aldens long to unpack. They were waiting for Violet to finish brushing her hair when Benny cried, "Look!" He was peering through one of the fan-shaped windows.

Jessie could tell by her little brother's face that something had startled him. "What's going on, Benny?" she asked, stepping up beside him.

"Look down there!" Benny said, his eyes wide.

"What is it?" Henry hurried over, with Violet close behind.

"It's a bridge!" declared Benny.

The Aldens huddled around, straining to see out into the gathering darkness. Sure enough, the shadowy outline of a curved stone bridge could be seen in a far corner of the backyard.

"There must be a creek behind the house," noted Henry.

Violet said, "I can't be sure, but I think

that's the bridge that was in the newspaper."

"Got to be," said Jessie. "That's the one Spence Morton wants to buy. I'm sure of it."

Benny nodded. "I bet it's the haunted bridge Darlene was talking about. We're not supposed to go fishing from it, remember?"

"Of course we can go fishing from it, Benny," Henry insisted. "The bridge isn't haunted."

"No one goes fishing from that bridge," said a voice behind them. "No one does. Ever."

CHAPTER 2

A Strange Verse

Henry, Jessie, Violet, and Benny turned around quickly in surprise. A young girl about Violet's age was standing at the opened door, watching them. She was wearing jeans and a green T-shirt. Her blond curls were held back from her face with a beaded headband.

"You must be Pam," Jessie said with a friendly smile.

"That's right. And you must be the Aldens."

"Yes. I'm Jessie, and this is Henry, Benny,

16

and Violet." Jessie motioned to her brothers and sister in turn.

"I don't get it," said Henry. "Why doesn't anyone go fishing from—"

Before Henry could finish his thought, Pam wheeled around and walked off.

The Aldens looked at one another in confusion. "Pam sure seemed in a hurry to get away," Violet said with a puzzled frown.

"I guess she didn't want to talk about the bridge," said Jessie. "I wonder why."

Henry shrugged. "Beats me."

"I bet it *is* haunted," Benny said in a hushed voice. "I just bet!"

* * * *

"Help yourself to more meatballs, Benny," Norah urged at dinner.

The youngest Alden didn't need to be coaxed. "Thanks," he said, eagerly adding a few more to his plate of spaghetti.

Mrs. McGregor turned to Norah's great-niece. "You've really grown since I saw you last, Pam," she said with a warm smile.

"Time sure flies, doesn't it?" Norah took the basket of garlic bread that Violet handed her. "Pam was only a toddler when she spent her first summer with me." Norah reached out and gave her niece an affectionate pat on the arm.

Violet looked over at Pam. "You must miss your parents."

Pam's face turned red and she lowered her eyes.

"We miss Grandfather whenever he goes away on business," Benny chimed in as he wiped tomato sauce from his chin.

Pam looked glumly at her plate. "Who needs parents around all the time?"

The Aldens were surprised by her words, but they didn't say anything.

Just then, a young woman in a yellow halter top and matching shorts came into the room. She was very tall with lots of curly brown hair. "Sorry I'm late, Norah," she said, slipping into an empty chair beside Jessie. "I lose all track of time when I'm working."

"Not to worry," Norah said with a cheery smile. "Everything's still piping hot." Then she introduced Mrs. McGregor and the Aldens to Annette Tanning. "Annette's helping me research the Eton family. She's from out-of-state, so she'll be staying here until school starts again in the fall."

"You're in college, Annette?" Jessie asked, passing the salad along.

"Yes, I'm studying history." Annette placed a napkin over her lap. "When I saw Norah's ad for a research assistant, I jumped at it."

Norah smiled. "I was lucky to get such a hard worker."

"I really love looking through old things," Annette went on. "You never know what treasures you'll find."

That got Benny's attention. "You found a treasure?"

"Not a real treasure." Annette laughed nervously. "Nothing like that. Just interesting facts. That's all I meant about—" She stopped suddenly as if she knew she'd said too much.

Benny polished off his milk. "We're good at finding real treasures," he said proudly. "Right, Henry?"

"We have found a few," Henry admitted.

Seeing Annette's puzzled face, Mrs. McGregor explained, "These children are first-class detectives."

"Detectives?" Pam looked over in surprise.

"We solve mysteries," Benny told her with a grin. "That's our specialty."

Norah turned to her assistant. "I think we have just the mystery for them. Right, Annette?"

"What...?" Annette held her fork in mid-air. "What are you talking about?" She sounded upset.

"Why, Meg Plum's mystery, of course," answered Norah. "What else?"

Suddenly Annette's whole manner changed. "If you don't think *I'm* doing a good job, Norah, just say so!" She stabbed at a meatball with her fork.

The Aldens were surprised. They stared at Annette with their mouths open.

"Of course I think you're doing a good job." Norah looked shocked. "What's gotten into you, Annette?"

"Well, for starters, I can't work with a

bunch of kids in the way."

Benny put down his fork. "But we never get in the way."

Mrs. McGregor was quick to agree. "The Aldens are very self-reliant."

"Of course they are," agreed Norah. "No reason for anyone to be upset." But it was clear that Annette was upset.

"We'll do our best to help," Henry promised.

"Thank you, Henry," said Norah.

Annette looked as if she wanted to argue. But she didn't. She finished her dinner in silence, not looking too pleased. Then she excused herself and left the room.

Norah apologized for her assistant's behavior. "Annette has many good qualities, but she can be a bit moody sometimes."

When the Aldens were clearing the table, Henry let out a low whistle. "Annette sure doesn't want us helping out," he said.

Benny added, "She wasn't very friendly."

"I guess we'd better keep out of her way," said Jessie, filling the sink with hot, soapy water. The children agreed.

After leaving the kitchen spic-and-span, the four Alden children hurried out to the front porch. Norah and Mrs. McGregor were sipping iced tea and chatting. Pam was bent over a jigsaw puzzle nearby. Annette was nowhere in sight.

The Aldens made themselves comfortable. Then Benny looked at Norah—was she ready to tell them about the mystery?

Norah was ready. She took a last sip of her iced tea, then placed the empty glass on the table beside her. In the soft glow of the porch light, with the crickets singing in the dark, she began telling them an odd tale.

"A long time ago, my great-great-grandfather, Jon Eton, decided to see a bit of the world. His travels took him to England, and to the little village of Stone Pool. That's where he met and fell in love with the beautiful Meg Plum."

"That's why your house is purple, right?" put in Violet. "Because of Meg Plum, I mean."

Norah looked surprised that Violet knew that. "Right you are, Violet," she said.

"Meg left the village of Stone Pool behind to start a new life with Jon right here at Eton Place. But I'm afraid my great-great-grandmother didn't have an easy time of it."

Jessie looked questioningly at Norah. "You mean, she didn't like it here?"

"Oh, she liked it well enough, Jessie. But she was terribly homesick. Apparently, she would sit for hours, just staring at a photograph of Stone Pool." Norah shook her head sadly. "They say Jon often found his young wife in tears."

"Poor Meg!" Violet was shy, and meeting new people often made her nervous. "Did Jon try to help her?"

"Yes, but I'll tell you about that another time, Violet." Norah was reaching for a photograph album from the table beside her. "Right now, I have something to show you. It just so happens Annette came across a photograph the other day." She pointed at a page in the album. "Here it is—Meg's photograph of the village of Stone Pool."

Although it was cracked and badly faded with age, the photograph showed shoppers

in old-fashioned clothes strolling along the walkways and in and out of the little stores. Benny pointed to the fancy script at the bottom of the photo.

"What does that say, Norah?" he wanted to know. The youngest Alden was just learning to read.

Norah put on her glasses and read the words aloud: "The village of Stone Pool as it appeared on a summer afternoon in 1810."

Mrs. McGregor peered over Norah's shoulder. "Looks like a charming village. No wonder Meg was homesick."

Norah continued her story. "One day, a special gift arrived for Meg from her grandmother."

The Aldens were instantly curious. "What was it?" said Henry.

"A heart-shaped brooch," Norah told them. "It was a family heirloom made from precious gems. The rubies were particularly beautiful and rare."

"What's a brooch?" asked Benny.

"It's a pin, Benny," Mrs. McGregor

answered. "Just like the one I have on my blouse. Only Meg's brooch sounds much fancier than mine."

"Meg loved the brooch. She wore it whenever she was feeling homesick." Norah started flipping through the pages of her album again. She stopped and pulled out an old photograph. "Here's a picture of my great-great-grandmother wearing her brooch." She passed it along.

Sure enough, the fair-haired woman in the high-necked blouse and long skirt was wearing a heart-shaped brooch at her throat. The Aldens took turns studying it— first Violet, then Benny, then Henry, and finally Jessie.

"I wish I could show you the brooch itself," said Norah, taking the photograph that Jessie handed her. "But I'm afraid that's impossible."

"Impossible?" Jessie looked puzzled.

Norah let out a sigh. "Sadly, the brooch disappeared long ago."

"Oh, no!" cried Violet.

"Apparently, Meg left the heart-shaped

brooch on her dresser one evening," Norah explained. "In the morning, it was gone."

Benny's mouth dropped open. "You mean . . . somebody stole it?"

"That's what everybody figured," said Norah. "But the strange thing is, they say there was no sign that someone had broken into the house."

"There's something I don't understand," Henry remarked. "Why would Meg leave a valuable heirloom out on her dresser in the first place?"

Jessie had been wondering the same thing. "If the brooch meant so much to her, why didn't Meg put it away in a safe place?"

"Exactly—yes!" said Norah, who seemed delighted by their questions. "It doesn't make sense, does it?"

Henry raised an eyebrow. "What are you saying, Norah?"

"I'm saying that I don't think the brooch was stolen." Norah closed the album and placed it on the table beside her. "I've always believed Meg found a secret hiding place for it."

Jessie blinked in surprise. "Why would she do something like that?"

"It's not as strange as you might think, Jessie." Norah settled back against a cushion. "I'm just guessing, but it's possible she hid that brooch to keep it safe—and out of her husband's reach."

"What do you mean?" asked Violet.

"Now, don't get me wrong," Norah said, holding up a hand. "Jon Eton was a kind man, but he liked to gamble. He was a bit too interested in money for his own good."

"Interested enough to sell Meg's brooch?" Jessie asked in surprise.

"It's hard to say, Jessie. But I don't think Meg was taking any chances. I'm convinced she found a hiding place for it."

"How can you be so sure, Norah?" Henry wondered.

"Because in her later years, Meg made a wall-hanging with a verse hand-stitched on it." Norah leaned forward. "I believe that verse holds a secret."

"What kind of secret, Norah?" asked Henry, unable to keep the excitement out of his voice.

"The secret of where the brooch is hidden." Norah reached down for the framed verse propped against her chair.

"Oh, it's beautiful!" Violet cried as Norah held it up for everyone to see.

Jessie moved closer to get a better look. "Meg used a different-colored thread for every letter," she said admiringly.

Norah smiled proudly. "Meg was known for her fancy stitching."

Benny could hardly stand the suspense. "What does it say, Norah?" he asked, bouncing up and down. "The verse, I mean."

Norah smiled at Benny's enthusiasm. Then she read the words on it aloud:

> *When last goes first,*
> *and first goes last,*
> *Eton's Loop will show you*
> *a clue from the past.*

Confused, the Aldens looked at one another. After hearing the verse one more time, Henry said, "That's a tough one to figure out!"

Benny agreed. "It's not much to go on."

Jessie tugged her small notebook and pencil from her pocket. As she copied the verse, Henry and Violet looked at each other and smiled. They could always count on Jessie to be organized.

"I don't get it." Benny was thinking hard. "What exactly is Eton's Loop?"

"I wish I knew, Benny," Norah told him.

"When we were your age," put in Mrs. McGregor, "we drove ourselves crazy trying to figure it out. Every time we thought we were on to something—"

"We'd end up going around in circles!" finished Norah.

Violet had a sudden thought. "Would you like to work on the mystery with us, Pam?" she asked, looking over at her.

"We can use all the help we can get," added Henry.

Pam shook her head. "I don't like mysteries," she said, barely looking up from her puzzle.

Benny could hardly believe his ears. "But they're just like jigsaw puzzles," he was quick to point out. "You fit all the pieces together and—"

Before he had a chance to finish, Pam suddenly got to her feet. "I think I'll go up to bed."

Norah looked disappointed. "Well . . . I suppose that's best if you're tired. Oh, would you mind putting this back in the living room for me on your way, dear?" she added, holding the photograph album out to Pam.

"In the cabinet with the glass doors, right?"

"Right."

With that, Pam gave her great-aunt a hug, then she said good-night and went inside. Norah looked worried.

"Pam just hasn't been herself this summer," she said. "She's usually so cheery. For the life of me, I can't figure out what's bothering her."

The Aldens looked at one another, wondering the same thing.

CHAPTER 3

The Watery Ghost

That night, all the Aldens fell asleep right away. Around midnight, Benny stirred. He thought he heard something— a rushing kind of sound. It seemed to be coming from outside. What was making that noise?

"Henry?" he whispered.

Henry didn't answer. He was sound asleep.

Benny slid out of bed. He went over to the window. Leaning on the sill, he peered out through the window screen into the inky darkness.

The strange noise suddenly stopped.

"Benny?" Henry asked sleepily. "What's going on?"

"I . . . I heard something."

"It's just the crickets," Henry said in the middle of a yawn. "Nothing to worry about."

Benny nodded his head. "No, it was something else, Henry," he insisted, trying to keep his voice low. "Something . . . weird."

"You were probably dreaming," Henry told him, in a sleepy voice.

"Maybe," Benny said, as he climbed back into bed. But he knew he wasn't dreaming.

* * * *

"I'm telling you, your great-great-grandmother's brooch was stolen," Annette was telling Norah at breakfast the next morning. "If you ask me, it was taken by one of the workmen at the time."

Benny frowned. "You don't think there's a secret hiding place?"

"I certainly don't." Annette tore a small piece of crust off her toast and popped it into her mouth. "I've done the research. I know what I'm talking about."

Benny looked crushed.

Violet felt her little brother's disappointment. "We won't know for sure until we do some investigating, Benny." She passed the platter of bacon to Pam.

Henry nodded. "We should at least check into it."

"Maybe you missed something, Annette," Benny said.

This was the wrong thing to say. Annette frowned. "Well, isn't it lucky we have the Aldens around to keep us on track," she said, though it was clear from her voice that she didn't think it was lucky at all.

Jessie and Henry looked at each other. Why was Annette so unfriendly?

"According to all the old newspapers, there was no evidence of theft." Norah took a bite of her toast and chewed thoughtfully. "And what about that little verse of Meg's? What do you think it means, Annette?"

"Nothing, probably."

Norah lifted an eyebrow. "Nothing?"

"Nonsense verse," Annette said, patting her mouth with a napkin. "That's all it is."

Pam tucked a loose strand of hair under her polka-dotted headband. "What's nonsense verse?" she asked.

"A silly rhyme that has no meaning whatsoever," Annette answered.

But Norah wasn't convinced. "I think there's more to Meg's verse than meets the eye."

Mrs. McGregor was quick to agree. "If anyone can figure it out, the Aldens can."

Annette threw up her hands in a frustrated way. "Well, I have better things to do with my time," she said, pushing back her chair. "I'll be in the den if you need me."

"Before you go, Annette," Norah said, changing the subject. "I was wondering if you've seen my tape recorder. It seems to have disappeared from my desk."

Jessie couldn't help noticing that Pam was blushing.

"I'm afraid not," said Annette. Then an

amused smile curled her lips. "But I'm sure the Aldens can track it down—just like that!" she added, with a snap of her fingers. Then she hurried away.

"I don't think Annette likes us," Benny said in a small voice. He wasn't used to anyone making fun of them.

"I'm sure she likes you just fine, Benny," Norah assured him. "She puts in long hours and it makes her a bit grumpy. You mustn't let it bother you." She paused as she swallowed a mouthful of eggs. "This research seems to mean a great deal to Annette. I'm not really sure why."

Mrs. McGregor, who was buttering her toast, suddenly looked up. "Your assistant seems sure the brooch was stolen."

Benny nodded. "By one of the workmen. I wonder what she meant by that."

"She was talking about the men who were working on the bridge," explained Norah, as she poured syrup on her pancakes. "They were hired around the time the brooch disappeared."

Henry asked, "Are you talking about the

bridge out back?"

"That's right, Henry," said Norah. "It came all the way from Stone Pool."

"Stone Pool?" Violet looked at Norah in surprise.

"It was the bridge where Jon proposed to Meg," put in Mrs. McGregor, as she helped herself to more bacon. "Right, Norah?"

Norah smiled at her friend. "Yes, indeed, Margaret! And Jon was determined to bring that bridge across the ocean for his bride."

Violet nodded in understanding. Jon wanted to bring a part of Stone Pool to Eton Place to keep Meg from feeling homesick.

"They say he made an offer that the village of Stone Pool just couldn't refuse. In no time at all, the bridge was taken apart, stone by stone, and shipped to America." Norah smiled a little. "There was only one problem."

"What was that, Norah?" Jessie asked.

"Jon was positive the bridge would span the stream in the woods," she said. "But he was sadly mistaken. You see, the bridge wasn't nearly long enough."

"At least the bridge was the right size for the stream behind the house," Violet pointed out.

"There's no stream running through the backyard, Violet." Norah said. "The bridge doesn't cross over water—only a large bed of pansies."

"No wonder nobody ever goes fishing from it," Henry realized.

"Not a drop of water under it," Norah said with a nod. "Never has been." She handed the syrup to Benny. "But Meg didn't mind," she added. "It made her happy to look out and see that old stone bridge in the backyard."

Benny was wondering about something. "Is the bridge haunted, Norah?"

"Darlene spilled the beans, I'm afraid," said Mrs. McGregor.

Norah rolled her eyes. "Darlene never did know how to hold her tongue."

The Aldens looked at one another in astonishment. Had Darlene been right after all?

"Does Jon haunt the bridge?" Violet wanted to know. "Or is it Meg?"

Benny suddenly remembered what Mrs. McGregor had said. "I bet it's the ghost of the chattering bones!"

Norah smiled over at the youngest Alden. "You hit the nail on the head, Benny!"

Jessie was curious. "Will you tell us more about it, Norah?"

Norah said, "Over the years strange noises have sometimes been heard in the middle of the night."

Benny's eyes widened. "What kind of noises?"

"I've never heard the noises myself, Benny," Norah said, as she padded her mouth with a napkin. "But they say it sounds just like water flowing over rocks."

The Aldens were so surprised all they could do was stare. Before they could ask any questions, Norah spoke again.

"You see, 'Chattering Bones' was the name of a little stream near Stone Pool. For many years it flowed under an old stone bridge on the edge of town."

Violet gasped. "The bridge Jon bought for Meg?"

Norah nodded her head. "The very same one that was taken apart and shipped across the ocean."

Pam, who had been quietly peeling an orange, suddenly looked up. "Just after that, the Chattering Bones disappeared."

"Disappeared?" the Aldens echoed in unison.

Pam nodded. "It vanished into thin air."

Henry was baffled. "But it couldn't just . . . vanish!"

"Apparently it did, Henry. They say the stream dried up shortly after the bridge was torn down. It was almost as if the creek needed the bridge." Norah spoke slowly as if uncertain about what she was saying.

Violet shivered. Everything was becoming more and more mysterious. Benny's eyes were round. "You mean, the sound at night is the ghost of the Chattering Bones?"

Pam was the first to answer. "Yes, the ghostly stream flows under the bridge when it's dark." Her voice was quiet, almost a whisper.

Benny's eyes grew even rounder. He hurried over to the window and peeked outside.

"That's a strange ghost story," Jessie remarked, as she got up to clear the table.

"Eton Place has its share of mysteries," Mrs. McGregor agreed. "No doubt about that."

Benny suddenly looked over at Norah. "That man's out there again."

"What man?" asked Henry, coming up behind his brother.

"The one who wants to buy the bridge."

In a flash, Norah was on her feet. "That fellow needs to be told a thing or two!"

Everyone followed as she led the way outside. Sure enough, they found Spence Morton standing on the bridge. He waved over to them. Spence was all smiles when they hurried over. "Just checking on my bridge," he told them.

"Now just what does that mean?" Norah had an angry frown on her face.

But Spence didn't seem to hear Norah. He just stared down at the stones and smiled.

"This bridge is mine," Norah said sharply. "And I won't be selling it to you or anyone else!"

Spence suddenly laughed, but not in a funny way. "I've got a hunch you'll change your mind," he said. Then he turned and strode away.

The Aldens exchanged worried looks. What was Spence Morton planning to do?

CHAPTER 4

Jon's Blunder

As Spence walked off, Benny edged closer to the rough stone ledge and peered over the side. Down below, purple pansies rippled in the breeze. He looked relieved.

As if reading his thoughts, Henry put a comforting arm around his brother. "Not a drop of water in sight."

"The Chattering Bones haunts the bridge at night," said Pam, who was standing within earshot. "Remember?"

Henry turned to look at her. "You don't really believe that, do you?"

Before Pam had a chance to answer, Jessie called out, "Look at this." She pointed to a small bronze plaque bolted to one of the stones. Engraved on the plaque were the words JON'S BLUNDER.

"One of the men working on the bridge had it made as a joke," Norah told them. "It wasn't long before everyone started calling the bridge Jon's Blunder."

Benny frowned. "What's a blunder?"

"A blunder's a mistake, Benny," Henry told him. "A big mistake."

"Oh!" said Benny, catching on. "And Jon made a big mistake—the bridge wasn't long enough for the stream."

Norah laughed. "I'm afraid my great-great-grandfather never heard the end of it."

Just then, Violet noticed something, too. The shape of a heart had been chiseled into one of the stones nearby. In the middle of the heart was Meg's name.

They all moved closer for a better look. "Jon carved that heart for Meg on the day he proposed to her," said Mrs. McGregor. "Right, Norah?"

"That's right, Margaret."

"It's so romantic," said Violet. She had a dreamy smile on her face as she traced the letters MEG with a finger.

But Benny was more interested in the mystery. "Let's get started looking for clues," he suggested.

"Any idea where you'll begin?" Norah asked as they headed back to the house.

"We thought we'd hike around the property," said Jessie. "Maybe keep an eye out for Eton's Loop."

"Whatever that is," added Benny.

Mrs. McGregor looked up at the blue sky. "Why not pack a lunch?" she suggested.

"Oh, yes!" put in Norah. "What could be better than a picnic?"

"Nothing!" cried Benny, who loved picnics.

Mrs. McGregor smiled. "There's a great spot to eat by the stream in the woods."

"Sounds good," said Henry.

"Come with us, Pam," Jessie offered.

Pam put on a little smile. "Thanks, but

I never hike that far. Not all the way to the woods."

The Aldens looked at each other, puzzled. How could anyone turn down a picnic?

As they went inside, Norah said, "By the way, there's a potluck dinner at the community center tonight, so watch the time."

"What's a—" Benny began to say, but Jessie knew the question before he asked it.

"A potluck's where everybody brings something, Benny," she explained. "That way, you get to sample different dishes."

Benny broke into a big grin. "Sounds like fun!"

"A picnic and a potluck dinner in the same day," said Henry. "That's a dream come true for you, Benny!"

The Aldens washed and dried the breakfast dishes, then made sandwiches on the counter. Violet buttered the bread. Henry added cold cuts, pickles, and lettuce. Benny slapped on the mustard. And Jessie cut and wrapped the sandwiches that Benny passed to her.

"I wonder why Pam never wants to do anything with us," said Benny, licking some mustard from the back of his hand.

"I'm not sure," Jessie said after a moment's thought. "She's hard to figure out."

"You've got that right," said Henry.

"She didn't even want to help us solve a mystery," added Benny, who still couldn't get over it.

"Maybe Pam's shy around new people," Violet was quick to suggest.

Jessie frowned as she wrapped a sandwich. She thought there was more to it than that. Pam always seemed so eager to get away from them.

Henry filled a large thermos with lemonade. "I think we should concentrate on one mystery at a time," he said, and the others nodded.

Jessie loaded their picnic lunch into her backpack. She even remembered Benny's special cup—the cracked pink cup he had found while they were living in the boxcar.

Then they filed out the door.

"Stick together!" Norah called out to

them from an opened window. "We don't want anyone to get lost."

"Don't worry, Norah," Jessie called back to her with a little wave. "We always stick together."

The Aldens set off across the fields, following a row of scraggly pines that grew near a rail fence. They made a detour around a weedy pond and stopped by a lone apple tree on a hill to pick wildflowers. By the time they reached the woods, the afternoon sun was getting hot and their flowers were starting to wilt.

"I'm starving," said Benny, as they followed a winding path covered with pine needles. "Is it lunchtime yet?"

"Got to be!" said Henry. "I'm ready for a break."

"Mrs. McGregor said there was a good spot for a picnic by the stream," Violet recalled.

"It must be up ahead," guessed Jessie. "Let's keep going a while longer."

Pine needles crackled under Benny's feet as he quickened his pace. "Sure hope we find it soon," he said, rubbing his empty stomach.

"Doesn't it smell wonderful here?" Violet said, looking back at her older sister.

Jessie filled her lungs with the spicy scent of pine. "It sure does."

Just then, Benny stopped so quickly that Henry almost bumped into him.

"What's wrong?" Henry asked.

Benny stood frozen to the spot.

"Benny?" Jessie said in alarm. "Are you okay?"

The youngest Alden put a finger to his lips signaling for the others to be quiet. "Listen!"

No one spoke for a moment. Then Henry nodded. So did Jessie and Violet. They heard it, too. A rushing noise.

"That's water rushing over rocks," stated Henry. "The stream must be close by."

It wasn't long before they reached a stream that wound its way through the woods.

They quickly made themselves comfortable on the grassy bank. Then Jessie passed out the sandwiches while Henry poured the lemonade.

"Mrs. McGregor was right," Violet said as she unwrapped a sandwich. "This really is a perfect spot for a picnic."

Jessie looked around. "It's a perfect spot for a bridge, too," she said, taking the lemonade that Henry handed her.

"You're right, Jessie," said Henry. "I bet this is just where Jon Eton was going to put that old stone bridge."

"I wonder if . . . " Violet began and then stopped herself.

"Are you wondering if one of the workmen really did steal Meg's brooch?" Jessie asked. "I don't blame you, Violet. I can't help wondering about that myself."

"Annette seems so convinced," said Violet.

Henry suddenly had a thought that hadn't occurred to him before. "Maybe it wasn't one of the workmen who stole the brooch."

"What are you getting at, Henry?" Violet looked confused.

"Maybe Jon took Meg's brooch."

"I suppose so." Violet frowned. She didn't want to believe Jon Eton would steal his wife's family heirloom.

"If only we could figure out Meg's verse," said Jessie. She pulled her notebook from her back pocket and read the words aloud one more time.

> *When last goes first,*
> *and first goes last,*
> *Eton's Loop will show you*
> *a clue from the past.*

But nobody had any idea what the verse meant. It still didn't make any sense.

Violet couldn't help noticing that her little brother was unusually quiet. She could tell something was troubling him. "Is anything wrong, Benny?"

Benny's eyes were fixed on the water flowing swiftly over the rocks. "I heard it last night," he said softly.

"Heard what, Benny?" Jessie asked.

"Water rushing over rocks!"

The others stopped eating and stared at him. "I didn't know what it was," Benny told them. "But now I do."

"You couldn't have heard this stream last night, Benny," Henry argued. "It's too far away from the house."

Benny shook his head. "It wasn't this stream, Henry. It was the ghost—the ghost of the Chattering Bones!"

"Oh!" Violet put one hand over her mouth in surprise.

But Henry wasn't having any of that. "There's no such thing as ghosts, Benny," he said for the umpteenth time. "Not even ghost streams."

Violet glanced at Henry. She knew her older brother was right. And yet, Benny's words still gave her a chill.

"Benny, are you sure you weren't dreaming?" Jessie wanted to know.

"I thought maybe I was," Benny admitted. "I even forgot all about the weird noise for a while—until we got closer to this stream." He looked over at his brother and sisters. "It wasn't a dream last night. I'm sure of it."

"There's only one way to settle this," said Jessie. "If it happens again, we'll all check it out together."

Violet added, "That's a promise."

"There must be an explanation for what you heard, Benny," said Henry. "We just have to figure out what it is."

Benny gave his brother and sisters a grateful smile. They always knew how to make him feel better.

After lunch, the four Aldens slipped off their socks and shoes and stood ankle-deep in the icy cold stream. The water was so clear they could see to the bottom. Side-stepping the rocks, they waded downstream. By the time they got back, their pockets were bulging with interesting pebbles.

When they stepped onto the mossy bank again, Violet spotted something half-hidden in the long grass nearby. "Look at this," she said, holding up a braided green headband.

"I bet somebody's looking all over for that," said Jessie.

"Pam always wears headbands," Benny pointed out as he put on his socks.

Henry nodded. "Maybe it's hers."

"Possibly," said Jessie. "But not likely."

Violet agreed. "Pam never hikes this far, remember?" She slipped the headband into her pocket, hoping to find the owner.

Henry looked at his watch. "I guess we should head back."

"Right," said Jessie, remembering the potluck dinner. "It's a long hike."

With that, the four children followed the path out of the woods, still no closer to solving the mystery. In fact, they didn't have the faintest idea how they were going to solve it. All they knew was that they had to try.

CHAPTER 5

The Bones Chatter Again

Benny was checking himself out in the hall mirror when Mrs. McGregor came down the stairs in a peach-colored dress. "Doesn't everyone look wonderful!" she said, smiling fondly at the children.

Henry, Jessie, Violet, and Benny were ready for the potluck dinner. Jessie was wearing a watermelon-pink dress with pearly buttons. Violet had changed into a lavender T-shirt and pale blue skirt with lace pockets. Henry wore a blue shirt and black pants. And Benny had on a short-sleeved white shirt and tan pants.

Just then, Pam came out of the kitchen holding a covered dish. The cream-colored headband in her hair matched her dress. Norah, in a ruffled blue dress, was right behind her.

"Pam made pasta salad for the potluck," Norah said proudly as they headed out to the car.

"Oh, do you enjoy cooking, Pam?" Violet asked.

Pam nodded. "I'm not very good at it yet," she said. "But I'm learning."

"Pam's being modest," Mrs. McGregor said as they pulled out of the driveway. "It just so happens I had a taste—and it was delicious!"

"It smells delicious!" Benny piped up from the backseat.

Pam, who was sitting up front between her great-aunt and Mrs. McGregor, turned around and smiled. "I'm making cookies tomorrow, Benny. You can help me decorate them if you want."

"Sure!" Benny was grinning from ear to ear.

Pam was being very nice to Benny,

Jessie thought.

"I was hoping Annette would join us," Norah said as they drove through the peaceful countryside. "She doesn't know a soul around here. I wanted to introduce her to a few people, but she said she'd rather work."

"You certainly have a dedicated assistant," Mrs. McGregor remarked.

Norah nodded, then she added, "By the way, if anyone comes across that tape recorder of mine, please let me know right away. Annette and I both use it for research."

"You mean, it's still missing, Norah?" Mrs. McGregor was surprised to hear this.

"I'm afraid so."

"We'll keep an eye out for it," Jessie promised. And the others nodded.

"Oh, Pam," Violet said, "speaking of lost things, are you missing a headband? A braided green headband?"

Pam whirled around. "Yes, did you find it?"

Violet nodded. "We came across it when we were out today."

"That's great!" said Pam. "It's my favorite."

The Aldens looked at each other. Pam said she never went into the woods. Why would she lie to them?

Just then, Norah pulled into the busy parking lot at the community center. "I wonder what everybody's bringing for the potluck," said Benny. He sounded excited.

"One thing's for sure," said Norah, parking in an empty space. "You'll be stuffed to the gills by the time we leave!"

Benny jumped out of the car. "Let's go," he said, heading for the door.

Henry laughed. "When it comes to food, there's no stopping Benny."

Inside the packed center, people were already helping themselves to the hot and cold food set out on a long table. Pam went over to add her dish to the others.

"Wow, there sure are a lot of potluckers here," Benny said as he looked around. "I hope they save some food for us."

Jessie smiled at her little brother and brushed her fingers across his hair. "Don't worry, Benny. I'm sure there's plenty to go around."

Norah put a hand to her cheek. "Oh, no. There he is again!" she said, keeping her voice low.

The Aldens and Mrs. McGregor looked at Norah, then in the direction she was staring. A man in gold-rimmed glasses was eating dinner at a small table in the corner. The man was Spence Morton!

"Never mind, now. We'll just keep out of his way," Mrs. McGregor told her friend.

Henry noticed that Benny was eyeing the buffet table again. "I think there's still plenty of food there, Benny," he teased.

Norah smiled at the youngest Alden. "Getting hungry?"

"Sort of," Benny said, looking at her expectantly. "Is it time to eat yet?"

Norah laughed. "Go ahead."

The Aldens quickly made their way over to the buffet while Norah and Mrs. McGregor mingled with the other guests. The children followed the line of people moving slowly around the table. After helping themselves to the different dishes, they carried their heaping plates to a small table and sat down.

"Mmm," said Jessie, digging in. "Have you tried Pam's pasta salad? It really is great."

Henry nodded. "I'll second that."

"Don't all look at once," said Violet, "but Spence Morton has company."

One by one, the other Aldens peeked over to take a look. Someone with gray streaks in her dark hair was sitting across from Spence. They seemed to be deep in conversation.

"Isn't that Darlene?" Jessie said in surprise, trying not to stare.

"You mean the lady from the gas station?" asked Benny.

Violet turned around slowly to take another glance. "Yes, I think you're right, Jessie."

"I wonder what that's all about," said Henry.

But they soon forgot about Spence Morton as Norah and Mrs. McGregor joined them, with Pam close behind. They all enjoyed a cheerful dinner together. Even Pam was all smiles.

Benny was just polishing off his second helping of chocolate cake when he spotted someone waving. "I think someone's trying to get your attention, Norah." He nodded in the direction of a man seated a few tables away.

"You're right, Benny." Norah smiled and waved, too. "That's Bob Ferber. He did the work on my house."

A young man of about thirty came over. He had sandy-colored hair and a golden tan.

"Good to see you, Norah!" He put out his hand. "And you, too, Pam."

"How are you, Bob?" Norah responded, shaking hands. Then she introduced Mrs. McGregor and the Aldens.

"I'm afraid I ate too much," Bob confessed, after saying hello to everyone. "I seldom get a chance to enjoy such great cooking."

Norah smiled. "I hope business is going well," she said. "I know it's been quite a struggle to get it off the ground."

"Oh, it's not as bad as all that," said Bob. "I'll have my bills paid off soon—then it'll be smooth sailing."

Norah seemed surprised to hear this. "That'd be an amazing thing to do in such a short time."

Changing the subject, Bob turned to the Aldens. "So, are you enjoying your visit with Norah?"

Benny nodded. "We're solving a mystery," he said, his eyes shining.

"Oh?" Bob looked startled.

"At least, we're trying to solve one," added Henry.

Norah laughed a little. "I'll have to tell you about that mystery sometime, Bob."

"Right." Smiling uneasily, the young man glanced at his watch. "Well, now, just look at the time. Guess I'd better be off. Good luck with the old mystery, kids," he said, seeming eager to get away.

Jessie stared after him, puzzled. Nobody had mentioned it was an *old* mystery. How did he know?

* * * *

That night, after the Aldens had gone to bed, Violet lay awake thinking about Eton's Loop. What in the world was it? All day they'd kept their eyes peeled for clues. But

they'd found nothing that would help solve the mystery. Was the answer somewhere in the verse itself?

> *When last goes first,*
> *and first goes last,*
> *Eton's Loop will show you*
> *a clue from the past.*

Violet, who knew the verse by heart, was repeating the lines to herself when she suddenly heard something. What on earth was that noise? What could be—wait! She recognized that sound!

Violet slipped quickly out of bed. She gave her sister a shake. "Jessie," she whispered. "Jessie, wake up. Benny was right!"

Jessie sat up in bed. "What...?" Her voice was thick with sleep.

"I can hear water rushing over rocks!" Violet cried, rubbing her arms to take away the chill. "Listen."

Jessie sat very still for a moment. Then she said, "Your ears must be sharper than mine, Violet. I can't hear any—oh!"

Violet looked at her sister. "You can hear it, too, can't you?"

Jessie nodded her head slowly. For a moment, she was too astonished to speak. But she quickly pulled herself together. She was out of bed in a flash. She went over to the window and looked out. All she could see was inky darkness.

"Do you think it's true, Jessie?" asked Violet, who had just come up behind her. "Do you think that's the ghost of the Chattering Bones?"

"I don't know what to think," Jessie admitted in a hushed voice. "But one thing's for sure," she added. "Something very definitely odd is going on!"

Violet looked at Jessie. Jessie nodded back. They were remembering their promise to Benny. It was time to do some investigating.

As they stepped out into the hall, another door opened. It was Henry and Benny.

"You were right, Benny," said Violet. "We just heard it."

"It's the ghost of the Chattering Bones," Benny stated. "Henry heard it, too."

"I heard something," Henry corrected as

he led the way downstairs. "But that doesn't mean there's a ghost out there."

When they got to the kitchen, Henry reached for a long flashlight that was hanging on a hook by the back door. Then he turned to his little brother.

"Are you sure about this, Benny?" he asked. "Are you sure you want to go out there?"

"I'm sure," Benny said bravely.

With a nod, Henry opened the door and they filed outside. Closing the door behind them, they tiptoed down the creaky porch steps. Then, with the beam of the flashlight sweeping across the grass, they made their way closer to the bridge—and to the sound of rushing water. Then Benny suddenly stopped. He had seen something the others hadn't.

"There's somebody up there," he whispered.

Sure enough, a shadowy figure was moving across the bridge.

Henry beamed his flashlight upward. "Who's there?" he yelled.

As the Aldens gave chase, Benny suddenly

tripped and went sprawling. The others waited while he scrambled to his feet. But when they raced off again, it was too late.

Whoever had been on that bridge had escaped.

CHAPTER 6

Eton's Loop

"I don't understand it," said Henry as they had a late-night meeting in the room that Violet and Jessie shared. "Someone's going to a lot of trouble to make us think the bridge is haunted."

Violet frowned. "Who would do such a thing?"

"And how?" Benny demanded.

"Beats me," said Jessie, who was sitting on the bed next to Benny. "But it sure sounds like water's flowing under that bridge."

"Do you think anybody else heard it?" Benny wondered.

"Not likely," said Henry. "Norah and Mrs. McGregor have rooms facing the front of the house. So does Annette."

"What about Pam?" said Benny. "Her room faces the back."

Jessie shrugged. "Maybe she's a sound sleeper."

"Or maybe she has heard it," suggested Violet. "She does seem to think the bridge is haunted."

Henry said, "There's another possibility."

The others turned to him, puzzled.

"Maybe Pam's behind the whole thing."

"Oh, Henry!" cried Violet. "You don't really mean that, do you? You can't suspect Norah's niece."

"We have to consider everybody," said Henry.

"But why would she want to play a trick on us, Henry?" Violet couldn't believe Pam would do such a thing.

"You know, I've been thinking about Pam," said Jessie. "She said she never hiked as far as the woods. I wonder why she lied to us."

"That was weird," admitted Violet.

"What I can't figure out," said Henry, "is why Pam would lie about something like that."

"Or why she'd try to scare us," put in Benny.

"Maybe it's her idea of a joke," offered Jessie.

"Well, if it's a joke," said Henry, "it's not a very funny one."

"You know," said Violet, "There's somebody else we might want to include on our list of suspects."

"You're thinking of Spence Morton, right?" guessed Jessie.

Violet nodded. "Maybe he figures it's the only way to get Norah to sell her bridge."

"You mean, by convincing her it really is haunted?" asked Benny.

Violet nodded again. "He said he'd do whatever it takes."

Jessie looked thoughtful. "It's funny that he was sitting with Darlene last night. I didn't think he knew anyone in town. He said he was just passing through."

"Maybe they're working together," Henry suggested.

"You think Spence and Darlene are partners in crime?" asked Jessie.

"Could be," said Henry.

The others had to admit it was possible. After all, it was Darlene who first told them about the bridge being haunted.

"I thought of someone," Benny said. "Annette."

Violet looked puzzled. "Annette's a suspect?"

"She's trying to scare us away," said Benny. "And you know why? Because she wants to find the secret hiding place herself!"

That made sense to Henry. "You might be right, Benny," he said. "Annette's whole attitude changed as soon as Norah mentioned we'd be working on the mystery."

"And that would explain why she insists the brooch was stolen," Jessie realized. "She doesn't want anyone else looking for it."

Violet raised her eyebrows. "You think

Annette wants to steal the brooch?"

"Could be," Henry answered. "Don't forget, the brooch is made from valuable jewels. Maybe she needs money for school."

Violet still looked doubtful. "I know Annette isn't very friendly, but that doesn't make her a thief."

"No, but it does make her a suspect," Henry insisted.

"I don't think we should jump to any conclusions," said Violet, "until we have more evidence."

Jessie nodded. "We'll keep our suspicions to ourselves for now. Let's try to figure a few things out on our own first."

On one thing they were in complete agreement—there were a lot of strange things going on at Eton Place.

* * * *

After breakfast the next morning, Norah and Mrs. McGregor set off for town to do a bit of shopping. After waving goodbye, Henry, Jessie, Violet, and Benny went into the backyard to do some investigating. Maybe the person who had been on the bridge last night had left a clue.

"Let's spread out," Jessie suggested. "That way we can cover more ground."

"Good idea," said Henry. "If anybody sees anything, shout."

"Don't worry," Benny piped up. "I'll shout really loud."

After making a careful search of the bridge, Henry walked over to where Violet was combing the bushes. "Any luck?" he asked.

"Not so far," Violet admitted.

"We checked out the flowerbeds under the bridge," Jessie said when she and Benny joined them, "but—"

"We struck out," finished Benny.

"Hi there, kids!" It was Spence Morton. He was coming around the side of the house. "Is Norah around?" He flashed them a smile.

Henry said only, "I'm afraid not."

Benny folded his arms. "And for your information, the bridge isn't for sale."

Spence held up a hand. "Whoa, I didn't come to pester Norah. I'm here to apologize."

"Apologize?" Jessie echoed.

"I put a lot of pressure on Norah to sell me her bridge," Spence explained. "I shouldn't have done that."

"And you tried to scare everybody!" Benny said accusingly.

"What...?" Spence blinked.

Benny said, "You made it look like the bridge really was haunted."

"No, I didn't do that!" Spence looked startled. "I know I made a nuisance of myself, but I'd never pull a stunt like that." He looked at each of the Aldens in turn. "I have children of my own," he added. "I'd never try to scare kids like that."

The Aldens looked at each other. They had a feeling Spence Morton was telling the truth.

Spence continued, "Last night, I had a chat with the lady from the gas station. She told me that Norah's great-great-grandfather, Jon Eton, proposed to his wife on that bridge. She said he had it shipped all the way to America as a special gift for his homesick bride."

"That's right," said Violet.

"The article in the paper never mentioned anything about it," Spence went on. "I understand now why Norah refused to bargain. How can you put a price tag on family history?" He paused to gaze admiringly at the bridge. "Please say goodbye to Norah for me. It's time I was heading home." With a cheery wave, he walked away.

"Well, I guess that rules Spence Morton out as a suspect," Jessie said, climbing the porch steps.

"It rules Darlene out, too," added Henry as they trooped into the kitchen.

Benny sniffed the air. "Something sure smells good in here!"

Pam was taking a tray of cookies out of the oven. She smiled over at the youngest Alden. "Ready to do some decorating?" she asked him. "See what I've got? Butternut frosting and sprinkles!"

Benny didn't need to be asked twice.

After washing his hands, he set to work while Pam started on another batch of cookies.

The other Aldens sat around the table and tried to make sense of Meg's verse.

Jessie opened her notebook and read aloud.

When last goes first,
and first goes last,
Eton's Loop will show you
a clue from the past.

Once . . . twice . . . three times she read the verse. But it was no use. They still didn't have the faintest idea what it meant.

Violet glanced over to where Pam was adding a drop of vanilla to the cookie batter. "Do you bake at home, too, Pam?" she asked. "For your parents, I mean."

Pam looked at Violet in a strange way. "Why do you mention my parents?" she said in a cold voice.

Violet sensed she'd said the wrong thing. "I just meant . . . " her voice trailed off.

Jessie and Henry exchanged a glance. What's that all about? the look seemed to say. No one was sure what to say next. Then Pam dashed out of the room.

"That was odd," Jessie said, keeping her voice low.

Henry agreed. "Pam sure doesn't like talking about her parents."

"It does seem that way," admitted Violet.

As everyone gathered round to admire all the cookies, Benny said, "See the star-shaped one I decorated for Pam? Her name's on it."

Jessie tried to hide a smile when she saw where he was pointing. "You got the letters mixed up, Benny. You spelled MAP, not PAM."

The youngest Alden smacked his forehead with the palm of his hand. "Oops!"

"The letter M goes last, Benny," explained Violet. "And the letter P goes first." Benny scraped off the sprinkles and tried again. This time, he spelled Pam's name just right. Everyone cheered—everyone except Jessie, who wasn't paying attention. She had the weirdest feeling she was close to figuring out the puzzle, but she couldn't quite get hold of it. And then—in a flash—everything made sense.

"Of course!" she cried.

CHAPTER 7

Going . . . Going . . . Gone!

"Don't keep us in the dark," pleaded Violet. "What are you thinking?"

Jessie pointed to Pam's name spelled out in sprinkles. "See that?"

Henry nodded.

"Remember the first two lines of Meg's verse?"

"Sure," Benny told her. "We've read it about a hundred times."

Jessie went over to the table where she'd left her notebook. Pulling up a chair, she printed the words ETON'S LOOP on a blank page. With her pencil poised over her notebook, she recited, "When last goes first, and first goes last."

The others stared at her. They looked totally confused.

"I don't get it," Violet said as they sat down.

"That makes two of us," Benny said.

Henry added, "Three of us."

"I'll do the same thing Benny did," Jessie told them. "I'll switch the letters around."

She paused to look at everyone, hoping they'd see what she was driving at. "I'll make the first letter in each word go last, and the last letter go first." Jessie held up her notebook for the others to see—ETON'S LOOP had become STONE POOL!

"Oh, my goodness!" Violet said, putting her hands to her mouth.

"Wow!" said Henry. "That's good detective work, Jessie."

"I helped, too," put in Benny, who was busy scraping the last of the frosting from the bowl.

"You sure did." Jessie nodded. "You gave me the idea when you switched the letters around in Pam's name."

"What I can't understand," said Violet, "is what the village of Stone Pool has to do with the mystery."

"That's what we're going to find out," stated Henry.

Benny licked some frosting from a corner of his mouth. "How will we find out?" he wanted to know.

Henry thought about this. "Maybe the answer's in that photograph of Stone Pool. The one that Norah showed us."

Violet's eyebrows rose. "I hadn't thought of that."

"Let's keep a lid on this for now," Jessie suggested. "If it turns out we're on the wrong track, Norah's bound to be disappointed."

Just then, Annette poked her head into the kitchen, a pencil stuck behind her ear. "Hey, there!" she said, smiling as if glad to see them. "Do you mind if I join you?"

The children stared at Annette, wondering why she was suddenly so cheery and friendly.

Without waiting for an answer, Annette stepped into the kitchen, shutting the door behind her. "So . . . how are you making out with the old mystery?" she asked, giving them a big smile.

"Well, we figured out that . . ." Benny stopped talking in mid-sentence. He suddenly remembered not to talk about the mystery.

Annette was instantly curious. "Go on," she urged, as she pulled up a chair and set her coffee cup down on the table.

The children looked at one another. They didn't want to lie, but they also knew it was best not to discuss the mystery just yet.

"We have a lot of questions," said Jessie, "but not many answers."

Annette began to tap her pencil on the table. "Surely you've figured out a clue by now."

"A clue?" asked Jessie.

Annette sat back in her chair, looking at Jessie. Then, without another word, she got to her feet, grabbed her coffee cup, and marched out of the room.

When the door had closed behind her, the Aldens breathed a sigh of relief. "Can you believe it?" said Jessie. "One day she's making fun of us for being detectives, and the next she's—"

"Pumping us for information," finished Henry. "How weird is that?"

"Maybe we should forget about Annette for now," advised Violet. "We have a mystery to solve, remember?"

"You're right, Violet," said Jessie. "Time to check out the photograph of Stone Pool. I'm sure Norah won't mind."

"The album's in a cabinet somewhere in the living room," Benny recalled. "At least, that's where Pam was supposed to put it."

Sure enough, the Aldens found the album on the bottom shelf of an old pine cabinet with frosted glass doors. They made themselves comfortable on the sofa, then leafed through the album until they came to the old photograph. Jessie read the words at the bottom aloud one more time. "The village of Stone Pool as it appeared on a summer afternoon in 1810."

"That's funny," Violet said, looking over Jessie's shoulder. "The date's been under-lined three times." She wasn't sure but she thought it might be some kind of clue.

But Jessie had a feeling the photograph itself contained a clue. She held it at arm's length, tilting her head to one side and then the other. "I don't get it," she said at last. "I can't spot anything unusual, can you?" She passed the photograph to Henry.

Henry bent over to examine it. "It's just a picture of a village in the olden days. Nothing strange about it." He passed the photograph to Benny.

"I can see lots of people going in and out of stores," observed Benny. "Nothing strange about that, either."

Violet took the photograph that Benny handed her and studied it closely. "There's something wrong here," she said. "But I can't figure out what it is."

"There must be something we're not seeing," said Jessie.

But Henry was having second thoughts. "Maybe we're on the wrong track."

Without taking her gaze off the photograph, Violet said, "I think we're on the right track, Henry. I've got a strong hunch about it."

"Well, right now we're going nowhere fast," Henry pointed out.

"And I think better on a full stomach," added Benny.

Henry grinned. "We get the hint, Benny. Let's get some lunch."

"We'd better not take the photograph into the kitchen with us," Jessie said. "We might get food on it."

As Jessie placed the photograph on the coffee table, she thought she heard something—a slight shuffling sound in the hall. Was it just her imagination? Or was someone listening to them?

* * * *

Violet swallowed a mouthful of soup. "It's so strange."

"What's strange, Violet?" Henry asked, helping himself to a grilled cheese sandwich.

"I can't put it into words, but there's something about that photograph of Stone Pool that bothers me."

"It's a really old photograph, Violet," Benny pointed out. "It's kind of faded."

"That's true, Benny." Violet poured more lemonade. "It's more than that, though. I can't quite put my finger on it, but something's not right."

"When it comes to mysteries," Jessie said, "your hunches are seldom wrong, Violet. We'll check it out again after lunch."

After the delicious cookies had been sampled, and the dishes done, the Aldens made a beeline for the living room.

"Where's the photograph of Stone Pool?" Benny demanded.

"It's gone!" Jessie said. "It ought to be right here on the coffee table."

Violet nodded. "I remember seeing you put it there."

"Then...what happened to it?" asked Henry, glancing around in bewilderment.

Violet had a thought. "Maybe somebody put it back in the album."

"I sure hope that's the explanation," said Jessie. She quickly checked it out, but it was no use. The photograph of Stone Pool wasn't there.

"I can't believe it," said Violet. "Who could have taken it?"

"A thief—that's who!" declared Benny. "And it looks like an inside job. I don't see any broken windows."

This made Henry smile a little. "Let's not jump to any conclusions, Sherlock."

"I bet Annette stole it," said Benny, who wasn't about to let go of his idea.

Jessie looked over at her little brother. "We shouldn't suspect people, Benny, until we're certain it was stolen."

With that, they walked slowly around the room, checking behind cushions and under chairs. But the photograph of Stone Pool had disappeared.

CHAPTER 8

What's Wrong with This Picture?

The moment Norah and Mrs. McGregor came through the door, Jessie told them about the missing photograph. "I'm so sorry, Norah," she said. "I know how much it meant to you. I just don't understand what happened."

"Oh, dear," said Mrs. McGregor, in a concerned voice. "First the tape recorder, and now the photograph. What more can happen?"

"Don't you worry," Norah said kindly, patting Jessie's arm. "It just so happens I made copies to give out to relatives."

"Oh!" The frown left Jessie's face.

"Besides," Norah added as she started up the stairs behind Mrs. McGregor, "it's bound to show up. After all, it has no value to anyone but the family."

The Aldens exchanged a look. Norah didn't realize the photograph could be an important piece of the puzzle. It had value to anyone who was after the brooch.

"There's at least a dozen copies in my desk drawer," she called down to them. "The den's at the end of the hall, kids. Go in and help yourself."

"Let's check it out," said Jessie, who was back to her usual cheery self.

With that, the four children headed along the hall. As they got closer to the den, they noticed the door was open a few inches. They heard a familiar voice.

"I'm telling you, it's a foolproof plan." This was Annette speaking. "Nobody suspects a thing."

The Aldens didn't like the sound of this. They knew it wasn't right to eavesdrop, but in this case, they felt they were doing it for a good cause.

"No...they won't be a problem anymore," Annette was saying. "What's that?...We'll leave no stone unturned?" She was laughing loudly now. "That's a good one!"

"Did you hear that?" Jessie asked the others, as they walked back along the hall.

Henry nodded. "It sounds like Annette's up to something."

"And she was asking about the mystery today, too," added Jessie. "That's kind of fishy, don't you think?"

"It was suspicious," admitted Violet.

Benny looked over at his brother and sisters. "Shouldn't we warn Norah?"

"It is a pretty strong case against Annette," admitted Violet. "But we can't be sure what she was talking about on the phone."

Henry agreed. "And Norah would never believe she was up to anything—not without hard evidence."

"You're right, Henry," Jessie said. "It's one thing to suspect someone. It's another thing to have proof."

* * * *

That evening, Norah, Mrs. McGregor, Pam, and the Aldens went to a baseball game and cheered for the hometown team. Even Pam couldn't help getting into the spirit of things. The game went into extra innings, and it was late by the time they finally returned to Eton Place.

After getting ready for bed, the Aldens got together for another late-night meeting. "I wonder who she was talking to on the phone," said Benny, still thinking about Annette.

Henry answered first. "Spence Morton comes to mind."

"You think Annette and Spence are working together, Henry?" Jessie asked in surprise.

"Could be," he said.

"Annette and Spence?" Benny repeated, not understanding. "But Spence left town, remember?"

"Maybe that's just what he wants us to believe," suggested Henry.

Violet thought about this for a moment,

then she nodded. "I guess it's possible he was trying to throw us off the track."

"Exactly," said Henry. "So nobody would suspect him."

Violet tucked her brown hair behind her ears. "Maybe it isn't the bridge he really wants."

"What do you mean, Violet?" Benny wondered.

"It's possible Spence is after Meg's brooch."

"Oh, I hadn't thought of that!" said Benny.

Just then, Jessie remembered something. She quickly told her sister and brothers about hearing someone in the hall outside the living room.

"Do you think somebody was spying on us?" Benny said.

Jessie had to admit it was possible.

"I wonder how much he—or she—over-heard," said Violet, sounding a little uneasy.

"Enough to know the photograph was an important part of the mystery," Jessie responded.

The others nodded. No one would go to the trouble of stealing the photograph unless they knew it would help them find the brooch.

Henry had something to add. "Remember Annette saying on the phone, 'They won't be a problem anymore'?"

Benny nodded. So did Jessie and Violet.

"You think Annette was talking about us, Henry?" Violet asked.

"Yes," said Henry. "I have a hunch she was."

"I guess she thinks we can't solve the mystery without the photograph," added Jessie.

Henry nodded. "It's possible she took it without realizing there were copies."

"There's something I don't understand," Benny said thoughtfully. "Annette was the one who found the picture in the attic, right? If she wanted to steal it, why didn't she just take it then?"

"Maybe she didn't think it was important at the time," offered Violet.

"First thing tomorrow we'll get hold of one of the copies." Henry stretched and yawned. "Right now I'm too tired to think straight." With that, they decided to call it a day.

When Violet climbed into bed, her thoughts turned once again to the photograph of Stone Pool. She still had the nagging feeling that something was wrong. But what was it? She tucked the thought in the back of her mind as she drifted off to sleep.

* * * *

In the middle of the night, Violet cried out, "That's it!" She sat bolt upright in bed as the answer suddenly came to her. "That's why it was underlined three times!"

"Hmm . . . ?" Jessie looked over at her sister.

"I just figured out what's wrong with the photograph!" Violet threw back her covers and jumped out of bed. "Come on, Jessie. This can't wait until morning."

After rousing Henry and Benny, Jessie and Violet led the way down to the den. Sure enough, they found copies of the Stone Pool photograph tucked into Norah's desk drawer.

"So, what's going on, Violet?" Henry wanted to know.

"Think about this," Violet said, as they sat down on a little sofa. "The photograph's supposed to be from 1810. Right?"

Jessie, who was sitting in a circle of light from the lamp, glanced at the words in the old-fashioned script. "That's what it says."

"The problem is," Violet told them, "photography didn't come into use until the 1820s!"

Jessie blinked in surprise. "Then the photograph couldn't have been taken in 1810."

Violet nodded. "Meg got the date wrong."

"That's kind of weird." Benny wrinkled his forehead. "Do you think we found another clue?"

"I sure do!" Henry slapped Violet a high-five. So did Jessie and Benny.

"But...what does it mean?" put in Benny.

Nobody said anything for a while. They were all lost in thought. Finally Henry spoke up. "Are there any other mistakes?"

"I'm not sure," Violet said. "That was the only thing I noticed."

Bending over the photograph, Henry said 'hmmm' several times.

"What do you see?" Jessie asked, looking over his shoulder.

Henry didn't answer.

"Henry?" Jessie asked again.

"This is getting weirder and weirder." He ran his finger under the words in white ink. "It says the photograph was taken in the afternoon."

"What's weird about that, Henry?" asked Violet.

"The clock tower in the background says ten o'clock. The photograph couldn't have been taken in the afternoon. It was taken in the morning!"

"You're right, Henry," Violet cried.

"I just noticed something else." Jessie looked up from the photograph. "There's no way this picture was taken in the summer."

"What makes you say that, Jessie?" asked Violet.

"Look at the trees."

With their heads close together, the others took another look.

"No leaves!" Benny exclaimed in amazement. "The trees are bare."

"And there's smoke coming from the chimneys," added Henry. "Did you notice?"

Violet bent closer. "Now that you mention it . . . "

"Let's go over everything." Henry ticked off what they knew on one hand. "This picture wasn't taken in the afternoon. It wasn't in the summer. And it wasn't 1810."

The children looked at one another. How did Meg get so much wrong?

"I guess Jon Eton wasn't the only one who made mistakes," Benny pointed out.

"Jon Eton?" Henry gave his little brother a questioning look.

"He made a mistake about the bridge," Benny explained. "Remember?"

The Aldens suddenly stared at each other. "Jon's Blunder!" they all cried out in unison.

"I can't believe it!" said Violet. "Meg made all these mistakes on purpose. Her blunders were supposed to point the way to the bridge!"

"It all adds up," said Jessie. "Norah said the brooch disappeared around the time the men were working on the bridge. We're lucky Benny mentioned Jon's Blunder."

"Do you think . . . " Henry paused for a moment to sort out his thoughts. "Do you think Meg's brooch is hidden behind one of the stones?"

Jessie bit her lip. "If so, we have a big problem on our hands."

"What do you mean?" asked Henry.

"Remember what else Annette said on the phone?" Jessie looked around at them. "She said, 'We'll leave no stone unturned'."

Benny nodded. "And then she laughed."

Violet caught her breath in sudden understanding. "She knows!"

"Knows what?" Benny looked confused.

"Annette might have meant that the brooch could be hidden somewhere in Jon's Blunder," Henry informed his little brother.

Benny's jaw dropped. "Uh-oh."

"That would explain Spence's interest in the bridge," Violet realized.

Jessie said, "There's only one thing to do."

The others looked at her. "What's that, Jessie?" Benny said.

"Find the hiding place first!" she said.

"Well, what are we waiting for?" The youngest Alden was already heading for the door.

CHAPTER 9

Thief!

As they stepped outside, Henry was about to say something when Benny grabbed his arm. "What's that?"

Everyone turned to see where Benny was pointing. At the top of the bridge, a light flickered and vanished. There wasn't time to decide what to do. On the spur of the moment, Henry clicked off the flashlight and they made a dash for the nearby bushes.

The children crouched in the long grass, their eyes fixed on the shadowy figures standing in the middle of the bridge.

The muffled sounds of conversation reached their ears, but they were too far away to make out what was being said.

Benny whispered, "Maybe it's Annette and Spence! They might be looking for the secret hiding place."

Before anyone had a chance to comment, they heard a noise—it sounded as if someone were hacking away at the bridge!

"Oh, no!" Violet's eyes were huge.

Benny jumped up to peer over the bushes, but Jessie stopped him in time. "Stay down, Benny."

"But...somebody's tearing the bridge apart!" he cried, almost shouting. "What should we do?"

Henry said, "I don't know what's going on, but I think it's time to find out."

"Let's get closer," Jessie suggested. "Maybe we can hear what they're saying."

Keeping down, they crept cautiously forward. Then in a sudden burst of speed, they raced for another cluster of shrubs.

"Can't you work faster?" someone was saying. It was Annette!

"Give me a break!" came a grumbling male voice. It was clear the man was jabbing at the mortar that held the stones together. "I'm doing the best I can."

"The mortar's old and crumbling," Annette was saying. "Should be easy enough to get that stone out."

The Aldens looked at each other in alarm.

"I'm counting on your hunch being right," the man said. "Everything depends on it."

"I'm telling you, that plaque's the final clue," said Annette. "The hiding place is right behind that stone."

Jessie looked at Henry. It hadn't occurred to them before, but it made sense. After all, didn't the clues lead to Jon's Blunder? Wasn't that the name on the bronze plaque bolted to one of the stones?

All of a sudden, the battering noise stopped. "I think the stone's ready to come out," the man said. "Keep your fingers crossed."

"Thief!" Benny shouted. In a flash, he

had scooted out from behind the shrubbery. There was no stopping him.

The time for action had come. Henry and Benny raced onto the bridge from one side, Violet and Jessie from the other. Annette whirled around so suddenly, she dropped her flashlight. It rolled along the bridge.

"Who's there?" she shouted, blinded by Henry's flashlight.

"The Aldens," Jessie answered.

"I should've known!" Annette said. "This has nothing to do with you." She made a shooing motion with her hand.

Henry looked her straight in the eye. "We're not going anywhere." Then he shone the flashlight's beam on the man nearby.

The Aldens could hardly believe their eyes! It wasn't Spence Morton. It was Bob Ferber!

"You're the man from the potluck dinner," Violet said in surprise.

But Bob Ferber paid no attention to the Aldens. Instead, he plunged his hand into the dark space where the stone had been.

"Nothing!" He turned around, empty-handed. "Absolutely nothing."

Annette's jaw dropped. "How can that be?"

"You tell me!" Bob shot back. "You always seem to know so much."

"This is all your fault!" Now Annette was almost shouting. "You and your crazy ideas."

Just then, the bare bulb over the back door flicked on. Norah and Mrs. McGregor rushed out, pulling their robes around them. Half-walking and half-running, they hurried over to the bridge.

"Well, what's all the fuss . . . oh, my . . ." Norah stopped and stared at the gaping hole where the stone had been.

"What in heaven's name is going on?" Mrs. McGregor demanded.

"They're trying to steal Meg's brooch!" Benny said accusingly.

Norah looked from Annette to Bob and back again. "You two know each other?"

Bob struggled to find something to say. "Uh, well . . . I, er . . . " Suddenly, he stopped talking. His shoulders slumped and he leaned against the bridge, looking defeated. "Annette Tanning is my cousin." He could hardly look at Norah.

"What . . . ?" Norah was too shocked to speak.

For a moment, Norah and her assistant just looked at each other. Then Annette suddenly wheeled around to face Bob. "The whole thing was his idea," she shrieked, pointing a finger of blame.

Norah threw a sharp glance at Bob Ferber. "What do you have to say for yourself, Bob?"

Bob opened his mouth several times as if about to speak, then closed it again. Finally he let out a sigh and said, "All right, it's true. I was after your great-great-grandmother's brooch."

Norah stared at him, open-mouthed.

"The truth is, I happened to come across an old letter," Bob confessed, "when I was working on your house, Norah. I guess it slipped through a crack in the floorboards a long time ago."

"Oh?" Norah raised an eyebrow.

"It was a letter from Meg Eton's grand-mother." Bob hesitated a moment, then plunged in. "The letter made it clear that Meg was planning to find a safe hiding place for her family heirloom—a brooch made from valuable gems."

"No wonder you knew it was an old mystery," said Jessie, nodding.

Bob gave a little half-hearted smile. "I guess I gave myself away, didn't I?" Then he continued with his story. "I figured it was just the answer I was looking for. I knew, somehow or other, I had to get my hands on that brooch. The only problem was—" He stopped talking.

"You couldn't pull it off alone, right?" Henry said, urging him on.

"Right," said Bob.

Jessie guessed what was coming next. "You saw Norah's ad in the paper for a research assistant, didn't you?"

Bob didn't deny it. "It started me think-ing," he said. "Annette was in the history program at college. If she got a job here, I'd have someone working on the inside.

It all seemed simple enough."

"I'm shocked at you, Bob." Norah looked grim. "How could you think of stealing from me?"

"I never meant to hurt you, Norah." He let out a weary sigh. "I was desperate. I ran out of money and I had bills piling up. My plan was to sell the brooch and make some quick cash. What could I do? My business was about to fold."

"That doesn't make it okay to steal," Mrs. McGregor said sternly.

"I know it was wrong, but I really couldn't see the harm." Bob shrugged a little, trying to make light of it. "After all, folks seemed to think the brooch had been stolen anyway. I figured nobody would be the wiser if I—"

"Really *did* steal it," finished Violet.

Bob nodded. "Turns out the joke's on me," he said with a hard laugh. "It seems the brooch *was* stolen—probably before Meg had a chance to hide it."

Norah shook her head sadly. "You're a bright young man, Bob," she said in a quiet voice. "Why steal? That's never the answer."

Bob didn't have a reply to that. He just walked away, his arms hanging limp at his sides.

Norah turned to her assistant. "You were really a part of this? I thought you were someone I could trust." She sounded more hurt than angry. "You tried to convince me the brooch was long gone. And all the time you wanted it for yourself."

Annette looked around. Everyone's eyes were fixed on her. "I've done a lot of things I'm not very proud of," she said, swallowing hard. "I actually wanted nothing to do with Bob's plan at first."

"But then you changed your mind," put in Jessie.

"I needed the cash. Besides, the research job sounded perfect. I figured I might as well try to find the brooch, too. Bob was going to split the money with me."

"That's why you were pumping us for information, wasn't it?" said Violet.

Annette nodded. "I had a hunch you might have figured out a clue."

"What about the photograph of Stone

Pool?" asked Henry. "Did you take that?"

Annette nodded again. "I was standing out in the hall and I heard you talking about the photo. I couldn't believe you'd pieced together so much. You're smarter than I thought," she added, looking around at them. "I was afraid you'd beat me to the hiding place."

"What you don't know," said Jessie, "is that Norah had already made copies of the photograph."

Annette looked surprised. "Well, I guess our plan wasn't really—"

Violet jumped in. "Foolproof?"

"Oh, you heard me on the phone, did you?" Annette sighed.

"Your plan almost worked," said Benny.

"Yes," said Annette. "Things were going nicely until you kids arrived. You don't give up, do you?"

"No," said Henry. "Not until we fit all the pieces of the puzzle together."

Jessie had a question. "There's one part of this mystery I still don't get," she said. "How did you make it sound like the

Chattering Bones was flowing under the bridge?"

Annette stared at Jessie, a blank look on her face. "I have no idea what you're talking about."

Norah had heard enough. "I won't be needing your services anymore, Annette," she told her. "Please pack your bags."

"I'm sorry I betrayed your trust, Norah," Annette said quietly. Then she hung her head and walked away.

CHAPTER 10

The Secret Hiding Place

"I just can't believe Bob and Annette would do such a thing," Norah was saying, as they sat around the kitchen table having a late-night snack.

"Some people!" exclaimed Mrs. McGregor, who was pouring milk for everyone.

Pam came over with a plate of cookies. She set them down on the table. As it turned out, she had alerted her great-aunt after hearing noises outside.

"I have a question," said Violet. "If it wasn't Spence who was trying to scare us

113

. . . and it wasn't Annette . . . then who was it?"

"It was me," Pam said in a small voice.

All eyes turned to her.

"You tried to scare us?" Violet asked in surprise.

"You're the one we were chasing the other night?" Jessie said at the same time.

Nodding, Pam sank down into a chair. "I . . . I'm really sorry."

"What on earth is this all about?" Norah looked at Pam in bewilderment.

Pam buried her head in her hands. "I thought my parents would come and get me if they heard about a ghost," she said, sniffling. Jessie quietly handed her some tissues.

"But how could . . . " Benny's eyebrows furrowed.

Pam lifted her head and looked at the youngest Alden. "You're wondering how I did it?"

Benny nodded. "It sounded just like water rushing over rocks."

"Wait a minute!" Henry snapped his fingers in sudden understanding. "You recorded the sound of the stream in the woods, didn't you? That's why we found your headband by the water."

Pam glanced sheepishly at her great-aunt. "I know it was wrong to take your tape recorder, Aunt Norah." Her voice wavered. "I'm really sorry."

Norah was too stunned to speak.

"You went outside in the middle of the night, didn't you?" Henry went on, watching Pam closely. "Then you played the tape back."

Pam didn't deny it. "I had it all planned before you got here." She could hardly look the Aldens in the eye. "But I hadn't counted on you being so nice."

"We were hoping we could be friends," Violet said quietly.

"You might not believe this," Pam said, looking sad, "but I'd already decided not to try to scare you anymore."

Norah hadn't said a word for a while. Now she spoke up. "I knew you were unhappy, Pam, but I had no idea why." She paused and sighed. "I still don't."

Pam twisted her hands in her lap. "I love

spending time with you, Aunt Norah, but . . . I miss my parents." Her face crumbled. "I just wish they wouldn't go away all summer."

"Have you ever told them how you feel?" Jessie asked.

Pam lowered her eyes, then shook her head.

"Maybe it's time you did." Norah put a hand gently on Pam's arm. "They're not mind-readers, you know. Why don't we give them a call first thing in the morning?"

"I like that idea," said Pam, giving her great-aunt a watery smile.

"I'm sure you're always in their thoughts," Mrs. McGregor added kindly. "And in their hearts."

Suddenly Violet's mouth dropped open and she almost spilled her milk. A wild idea was flitting through her head. "We have to go back!" she cried.

"Back...where?" asked Henry.

"Back to the bridge!" Violet was on her feet in a flash. She grabbed the flashlight and headed for the door.

Baffled, the others followed outside.

When they reached the middle of the bridge, Violet swept the flashlight beam back and forth. It finally came to rest on the stone with the shape of a heart in it.

"What's going on?" Henry asked, curiously.

Violet didn't answer right away. With a finger, she traced the name inside the heart—the name MEG.

"I don't get it," said Benny.

"When Mrs. McGregor said Pam was always in her parents' hearts, it suddenly hit me." Violet's eyes were shining. "Look at the name inside this heart."

Henry scratched behind his neck. "I'll not following you, Violet."

"Remember the first two lines of Meg's verse?" she said.

Everybody recited at the same time, "When last goes first, and first goes last."

Henry suddenly drew in his breath, catching on. "If you switch the letters around, then—"

"MEG becomes GEM!!" finished Jessie, her eyes wide.

"Oh, my!" said Norah. "Meg's brooch

was made from precious gems."

Henry said, "I think we just found the final clue."

"Wait right here," said Norah, heading for the house. She returned a moment later holding a screwdriver. "This is all I could find. But it should do the trick."

With that, Henry set to work. The mortar crumbled easily as he jabbed away at it. When the stone was finally loose, he put his hands on either side, then he wiggled and pulled with all his might. Slowly the stone came out, revealing a gaping hole.

When Violet shone the flashlight's beam into the opening, Benny couldn't stand the suspense. "Do you see anything, Violet?" he wanted to know.

"I'm afraid I can't—wait!" Violet said.

Everyone gasped when Violet removed a small rotted leather pouch from the hole. For a moment they all remained still, staring at the pouch. Then Violet held it out to Norah.

Untying the drawstring, Norah gently pulled out a small cloth bundle. Her eyes

widened as she unrolled the cloth to reveal a dazzling brooch. "Oh!" A broad smile spread across her face.

The Aldens let out a cheer. So did Pam.

"I've never seen anything like it!" exclaimed Mrs. McGregor.

"No wonder Meg wanted to keep it safe," Henry said.

Norah nodded. "But she didn't want it hidden away forever. So she left clues for her descendants to follow."

But something was still bothering Benny. "What about the Chattering Bones?" he said, puzzled. "Does it haunt the bridge? Or doesn't it?"

Norah put an arm around the youngest Alden. "Some questions can never be answered, Benny," she said. "There will always be mysteries."

"Well, guess what, Norah?" Benny said with a grin. "Mysteries just happen to be our—"

"Specialty!" everyone said together.